His name was Cole and he was the nephew of the famous Irish warrior, Finn McCoul.

So when King Cormac captured Finn McCoul and held him prisoner in his castle at Tara, Cole ran to Tara to rescue his uncle.

Cole sprinted past the guards at the gates of Tara so fast that they didn't see him – they just felt their cloaks swirl against their legs.

But the king had so many armed warriors gathered round Finn that one slim, fast-running boy couldn't free him.

So Cole disguised himself as a servant and crept up behind King Cormac while he was eating breakfast with his prisoner. Cole whispered in the king's ear, "What must I do to win Finn's freedom?"

Once the king had recovered from his surprise, he asked, "What could you possibly do for me, boy?"

Cole said, "I'll do anything."

The king grinned. "Then I'll free Finn, if you carry out one simple task for me."

The king said, "Bring me a breeding pair, one male and one female, of every wild animal and bird in Ireland by tomorrow morning. When I have all those animals and birds, I shall be a true king of all Ireland. Then I won't need Finn McCoul at my table and you can have him back.

"But if you can't bring me all the birds and beasts for a zoo of my own, I'll keep your Uncle Finn, lock him in a cage, and make a zoo out of him. In fact, if you take this challenge and fail at it, boy, then I'll lock you in a cage too. I'll make a zoo out of the two of you!"

Cole said, "Uncle Finn, you'll be free by tomorrow."

The king laughed at the boy's confidence, because he knew the task was impossible.

Finn smiled, because he knew about the magic in his nephew's feet.

7

Cole ran to the mountains, and fetched pairs of
eagles, hares and ravens, and all the beasts and
birds of the heights. He ran to the moors, and
fetched rabbits, deer and hawks, and all the beasts
and birds of the heathers.

He ran to the forests and fetched wolves,
woodpeckers and foxes, and all the beasts and
birds of the trees.

Then he ran to the loughs and fetched ducks, eels and herons, and all the beasts and birds of the fresh water.

He ran to the beaches and fetched cormorants, otters and gulls, and all the beasts and birds of the salt water's edge.

Then Cole ran so fast that he ran into tomorrow night and back again, and fetched out badgers, bats and owls, and all the beasts and birds of the dark.

Cole started to guide the animals and birds towards the king's castle at Tara.

But the wild creatures didn't want to go to the king's castle. They wouldn't walk on the narrow path in a straight line, however nicely Cole asked.

The hares ran to the north, but Cole overtook them as they leapt, and herded them back in line.

The ravens flew to the south, but Cole overtook
them before they were far off the ground and pulled
them down again.

The two foxes, right at the end of the line, were
the trickiest. They would wait until Cole was busy
with both feet running and both hands grabbing, then
they would split up and run in opposite directions. But
Cole always caught them, by an ear or a tail or the scruff
of a neck, and pushed them back into line.

Cole's feet were grazed and his legs were tired, but he finally herded the line of animals and birds right up to the castle gates just as the sun went down.

"I have a gift for the king," he called. "A breeding pair of each bird and beast in the land. I'll give these to the king and he will free my Uncle Finn."

"Not yet." The tallest guard shook his head. "The king gave us our orders. He doesn't want the birds and the beasts until tomorrow morning.
Bring them back at sunrise."

12

Cole looked down at the animals, poised on their paws to run off as soon as they got the chance. He said to the guard, "Even if the king has decided he doesn't want these animals as much as he wants my Uncle Finn, we made a deal. So these are now the king's animals, and I'm sure you don't want them to get cold or wet overnight. Do you have a stable or a barn I can keep them in?"

The guard grinned. "Oh yes. The king has arranged very comfortable beds for you all ..."

13

The guard showed Cole to a house outside the castle walls. It was a nice new house, warm and clean, with a fireplace and windows.

But it was a house with nine doors. Two at the front, two at each side, and three doors at the back.

And not one of the nine doors had a lock.

Cole herded the animals in, helped them settle down for the night, then went back outside to stand guard.

Cole stared at the house with the nine doors. Perhaps the animals wouldn't notice that the doors didn't lock, he thought. Perhaps the animals wouldn't realise that they could just push the doors open. Perhaps he could take a break from running and chasing.

He watched the house. He listened at the windows. There was silence and peace inside. Cole smiled.

But it didn't stay quiet for long. BANG! CLATTER! CRASH! All nine doors opened at once, and all the animals dashed out.

The hares and herons, pigeons and polecats, ducks and deer, all burst out of the nine unlocked doors.

And the stag ran right at Cole.

The stag's huge antlers and strong shoulders knocked Cole over. Cole tumbled to the ground, gasping for breath.

He lay still, listening to the hooves and paws and wings of the animals escaping.

But he also heard the hammering and clinking of the king's workmen building cages for him and his Uncle Finn.

So he leapt up.

He grabbed the birds
by their tail feathers
before they were far off
the ground. And a hawk's
claws scraped his hands.

He scooped up the tiny animals before they were out
of sight. And a mouse's teeth nibbled his fingertips.

He overtook the deer and the badgers and the wolves
before they reached the trees. And a rabbit kicked
mud in his eyes.

Last of all, he caught up with the two cunning foxes.
They just grinned at him, as if this was a game.

And he shut all the birds and beasts inside the house
of the nine doors.

But Cole knew those doors wouldn't stay closed.
So he took a deep breath and ran faster than he had
ever run before, to the top of the nearest mountain.
He ran faster than the wind, faster than thunder,
faster than a lightning bolt. He pulled nine rocks
from the summit and sprinted back down to the house
of the nine doors. He moved so fast, that when
he reached the house, the doors were only just
creaking open.

He pushed the mice in with his toes and wedged one door shut with a rock. He shoved the oxen in with his shoulder and wedged another door shut with a stone. Then he grabbed the pair of foxes by their back legs, one coming out the front and one coming out the side, and wedged those doors shut with boulders.

Finally, every door was held closed with a heavy rock.

No matter how hard the foxes and oxen and deer pushed, they couldn't force the doors open.
Cole sat down against the ninth door, rubbed his toes and yawned.

His eyes closed, his breathing slowed and Cole fell asleep.

Suddenly, under his bare toes, the earth began
to shiver and shift. He jerked awake, and saw
the two rabbits appear out of a dusty new rabbit hole.

And he heard...

The click click click of the woodpeckers pecking at the roof beams.

The flit flit flit of the bats flying up the chimney.

The scratch scratch scratch of the foxes learning to work the window catches.

Cole stood up and started chasing animals again. All ... night ... long.

When the sun came up, Cole called a line of tired animals out of the ninth door. He herded them through the castle gates into the courtyard, and he stood sternly over the foxes, as the king came out in his nightgown.

"Here they are, your majesty," said Cole. "A breeding pair of every animal and bird in Ireland. I wish you joy with them. Now give me back my Uncle Finn."

The king walked along the line of animals.
He frowned. He walked back along the line, counting
on his fingers. "I can't see any missing animals
or any missing birds. Perhaps nine doors weren't
enough. I need more cages, but for these beasts, not
for you and your uncle. I must let you both go free."

Cole leant down and whispered to the foxes. "I hope you had fun playing tag! But playtime's over. I'm not going to chase you any more. Once I'm out of that gate, if you all want to go home, I won't stop you."

Then he walked out of the courtyard with his uncle.

For one minute, the king gazed at the neatly matched pairs of birds and beasts in his courtyard. He imagined them all lined up in cages in his feasting hall.

But that was the only pleasure he ever got from them, because as soon as Cole was out of sight, the foxes ran for the gate, the ravens flew over the walls and the mice scurried into the grainstore.

And none of the king's warriors was fast enough to stop them.

Where was the only boy in Ireland fast enough to catch them and bring them back?

He was walking, arm in arm with his uncle, away from Tara.

As the birds flew above him and the animals ran past him, Cole waved.

Slowly.

29

COLE'S IRELAND

beaches

King Cormac's Castle

the house of the nine doors

lough

30

mountains

moors

forest

31

Ideas for reading

Written by Clare Dowdall, PhD
Lecturer and Primary Literacy Consultant

Reading objectives:

- identify themes and conventions
- ask questions to improve understanding
- draw inferences and justify these with evidence
- make predictions from details stated and applied

Spoken language objectives:

- give well-structured descriptions, explanations and narratives for different purposes

Curriculum links: Geography – locational knowledge

Resources: ICT for research and fact-file making, art materials for storyboards.

Build a context for reading

- Look at the illustration on the front cover and discuss what can be seen, can children identify all the different animals?

- Ask children what they think *The House of The Nine Doors* will be about and what kind of story it is?

- Read the blurb together and ask the children what they think might be special about Cole, and how the animals on the cover might be involved.

Understand and apply reading strategies

- Ask children to read pp2-3 and then describe what they have read. Support them to use vivid detail in their descriptions and refer to the story.

- Read pp4-5 together. Ask children to each make a prediction about the simple task King Cormac plans to set for Cole. Remind children to look at the front cover for clues.